Jasper
and Jess

First published in 2001 by
Franklin Watts
96 Leonard Street
London
EC2A 4XD

Franklin Watts Australia
56 O'Riordan Street
Alexandria
NSW 2015

A CIP catalogue record for this book is available
from the British Library.

ISBN 0 7496 4080 4 (hbk)
ISBN 0 7496 4081 2 (pbk)

Series Editor: Louise John
Series Advisor: Dr Barrie Wade
Series Designer: Jason Anscomb

Printed in Hong Kong

Jasper
and Jess

by Anne Cassidy

Illustrated by François Hall

W

FRANKLIN WATTS

LONDON•SYDNEY

Jasper and Jess were enemies.

Jasper liked to chase Jess

out of his garden.

Every day Jasper waited
until Jess appeared.

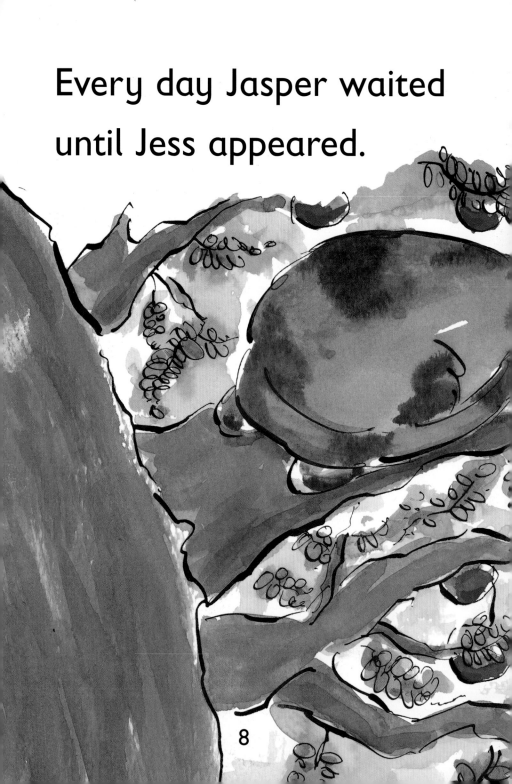

He chased her until she
ran up the apple tree.

He barked and growled
at her.

She arched her back and
hissed at him.

One day Jess didn't appear.

Jasper looked for her
behind the bushes and
in the flowerbeds.

He looked in the

rock garden ...

... and over the fence.

But Jess wasn't there.

Then Jasper heard a sound.
He looked up at the house.

Jess was stuck on the roof!

Jasper went to have a closer look.

Jess was hanging down
from the drainpipe!

Jasper ran up and down the garden, barking.

But no one heard him.

He scratched at the back door.

But no one was at home.

Quickly, he pulled a deck chair under the drainpipe.

"Jump onto the chair, Jess!" he shouted.

Jess was frightened but she closed her eyes and let go.

It was a long way down.

Jess fell through the air and landed on the chair.

She was safe!

Jasper was glad he had
helped Jess.

Now he could chase her out of his garden again!

Leapfrog has been specially designed to fit the requirements of the National Literacy Strategy. It offers real books for beginning readers by top authors and illustrators.

There are 25 Leapfrog stories to choose from:

The Bossy Cockerel

Written by Margaret Nash,
illustrated by Elisabeth Moseng

Bill's Baggy Trousers

Written by Susan Gates,
illustrated by Anni Axworthy

Mr Spotty's Potty

Written by Hilary Robinson,
illustrated by Peter Utton

Little Joe's Big Race

Written by Andy Blackford,
illustrated by Tim Archbold

The Little Star

Written by Deborah Nash,
illustrated by Richard Morgan

The Cheeky Monkey

Written by Anne Cassidy,
illustrated by Lisa Smith

Selfish Sophie

Written by Damian Kelleher,
illustrated by Georgie Birkett

Recycled!

Written by Jillian Powell,
illustrated by Amanda Wood

Felix on the Move

Written by Maeve Friel,
illustrated by Beccy Blake

Pippa and Poppa

Written by Anne Cassidy,
illustrated by Philip Norman

Jack's Party

Written by Ann Bryant,
illustrated by Claire Henley

The Best Snowman

Written by Margaret Nash,
illustrated by Jörg Saupe

Eight Enormous Elephants

Written by Penny Dolan,
illustrated by Leo Broadley

Mary and the Fairy

Written by Penny Dolan,
illustrated by Deborah Allwright

The Crying Princess

Written by Anne Cassidy,
illustrated by Colin Paine

Cinderella

Written by Barrie Wade,
illustrated by Julie Monks

The Three Little Pigs

Written by Maggie Moore,
illustrated by Rob Hefferan

The Three Billy Goats Gruff

Written by Barrie Wade,
illustrated by Nicola Evans

Goldilocks and the Three Bears

Written by Barrie Wade,
illustrated by Kristina Stephenson

Jack and the Beanstalk

Written by Maggie Moore,
illustrated by Steve Cox

Little Red Riding Hood

Written by Maggie Moore,
illustrated by Paula Knight

Jasper and Jess

Written by Anne Cassidy,
illustrated by François Hall

The Lazy Scarecrow

Written by Jillian Powell,
illustrated by Jayne Coughlin

The Naughty Puppy

Written by Jillian Powell,
illustrated by Summer Durantz

Freddie's Fears

Written by Hilary Robinson,
illustrated by Ross Collins